Invisible Influences

Jason E. Rolfe

Invisible Influences
by Jason E. Rolfe
ISBN: 978-1-913766-07-8

Cover Art by David Rix

Publication Date: April 2022

All text copyright 2022 Jason E. Rolfe

For Rhys Hughes,
a fine gentleman and a good friend.

Table of Contents

The Way of the Dead

Our memories are never etched in time. They are fluid and ephemeral, ever-changed by the life we've lived beyond them, and often what may have been an otherwise pleasant moment can be poisoned by future moments. Thus killed, the past becomes an imperfect ghost, haunting our memories like regret. Chased by these revenants I drove, through Plymouth and out, along the A386 toward Tavistock and gloomy Dartmoor beyond. Dartmoor, whose fogs and tors, flocks of sheep and cold stone prison lived and breathed beneath time's deceptive veil. Dartmoor, whose very existence was everything I imagined it would be and only vaguely like my memories of it. I drove on, following the Tavistock Road to Lydford and the medieval church it housed. The church, if I knew it at all, had been lost somewhere in the twenty-five years since we'd first met. I could still remember St. Michael's on the hilltop, Buckfastleigh, and Charles Church in Plymouth, its husk a scar left by the Nazi blitz. Though not by name, I could still recall the eight hundred year old church we'd visited one Easter morning, its moldering scent as strong in my mind as it had been that day; but the church in Lydford escaped me. I couldn't remember following in the footsteps of its flock along the ancient Dartmoor Forest path, from their farms on the moor to the church in Lydford. They called it The Way of the Dead because it was along this sun-dappled path that they carried their dead from the rolling, craggy moors to the cemetery gate.

The path ran over nineteen kilometres to a height of nearly four hundred and sixty metres. It was a challenging walk, far less so twenty-three years ago. Then, when everything was new and I was young, the experience made the journey worthwhile. Hindsight is blind, however, and the world had moved on from a moment two decades earlier when, through arrogantly naïve eyes, I gazed across Dartmoor, self-righteous in my youth. The view too had faded from my memory. I remember the stillness, the warmth of the tree-filtered sunlight, even the damp, earthy smell wafting lazily up from the forest floor to mingle with hints of bark and distant smoke drifting in the air above. Not the view. The image imprisoned in my mind was an amalgamation of various day trips through Devon and Cornwall, and Westcountry photographs I'd found online.

That was until I reach the stunted oaks and mossy stones of Wistman's Wood.

The sunlight, filtered by the oak leaves and the lichen that draped the gnarled and tangled branches overhead kissed the soft earth beneath my feet. The ghosts of Wistman's Wood awoke. I could hear their laughter, muted by time and memory. Were we so happy then because the world was new; or was it because we'd been shielded from the hardships of life by old oak trees and misty, tor-filled moors? The ghosts became clearer, wandering like shadows through the eerie forest. She'd slipped on a stone near the ruins of the old mill, landing with a wet smack in the shallow stream. I remember laughing, the red blush of her wounded pride. "Oh come on," I'd assured her. "You'll laugh about it later." I couldn't be certain, of course, but I doubt she ever did. Hers was always a self-esteem based on the perceived perceptions of others. The ghosts in Wistman's Wood were restless, their laughter, like mine, muted by the passage of time.

I sat down amongst the lichen-covered roots of an old oak and, with my back against its ancient trunk, closed my eyes and listened to the summertime silence. Twenty-three years ago, the silence had been broken by the sound of laughter unburdened by the weight of responsibility. The heavy anchors of adulthood had not yet been dropped and we were still innocently naïve enough to sail through life without the dragging stress of debt. Perhaps all love born within the utopia of youth is doomed to fail. Reality has a way of changing us, making us harder and far less romantic in our worldview. We can't sit amongst trees, savouring the stillness of our summers when we have bills to pay.

The gentle sounds stopped with a suddenness that raised the hair at the nape of my neck. The bees ceased their incessant humming, the birdsong fell silent. The breeze itself stopped kissing the hawthorn and the stunted willow and the trees stilled, as though holding their collective breath. The sounds I'd found comforting were replaced by an unfamiliar hymn, deep and mournful and sung in time with uncountable, moss-softened footsteps. People were approaching along the trail leading away from the moors and toward the Lydford church. Their voices, so solemnly gathered in song, startled the world around me into silence. I stood and awaited their inevitable passing. The song grew louder until I felt its somber rhythm in my chest as clearly as I felt their footsteps in the woodland detritus beneath my feet. I'm not sure how to explain what happened, or didn't happen, next, but when they reached the clearing I saw nothing. I felt their presence, was certain that if I'd reached out I would have touched them as they shambled past, but nothing disturbed my view of the lichen-covered oaks on the far side of the path. The dark and sorrowful song filled the clearing – yet I remained its only occupant.

In less than two minutes the invisible procession had passed. The song had faded its way up the trail toward the church and I was bathed in the silence of its absence. A buzzing bee sought the branches of a nearby hawthorn. A bird fluttered its wings within the concealing leaves of a neighbouring willow and the wind again breathed gently-swaying life into the oaken treetops. I shivered despite the summertime warmth. The unexpected chill chased me from my reverie and, picking up my shoulder pack, I followed the strange procession back toward Lydford.

The church was nestled in the surrounding greenery, as much a part of the landscape as the emerald hills around it. Although I don't remember visiting the church, or the village, twenty-three years ago, I did a cursory search before leaving home. I knew, for example, that the original church had been built in 649, and that it died at the hands (and torches) of the Vikings in 997. The church, dedicated to a Welsh monk named Petrock, was later rebuilt. Its mixture of Norman and Anglo-Saxon styles further suggested that today's church had been built upon an existing site. The tower was a fifteenth-century addition, while the vestry and the northern aisle were added in 1890. I couldn't tell you if I'd been inside the church; as I said earlier, memory is never etched in time. Sometimes I remember things that never happened as if they'd only happened yesterday, while I've forgotten things that actually did happen yesterday. I can't, for example, remember the name of the inn I'd checked into late last night. Less than five-hundred souls call Lydford home but I couldn't, for the life of me, remember the name of what was very likely the town's only inn. I couldn't remember how much I paid for the rental car in Plymouth, or into which pocket I'd placed the keys, but I could vividly recall a walk I'd taken through Wistman's Wood twenty-three years ago.

The cemetery was old. The headstones were listing heavily to one side or another and the church around which they marked the mortality of time was silent. It looked like countless other churches I'd visited during my various trips to England. Its silence was one of age and if one listened closely enough it seemed perfectly possible to hear long-forgotten lamentations to the dead. Those that I heard, far from being the somber dirge that drew me to this place, echoed with the laughter of lost youth. I could never explain the unseen procession that led me from Wistman's Wood, along the Way of The Dead to St. Petrock's Church, but I've often thought the corpse it carried with it was that of my youth.

The Last Moments of Daniil Ivanovich

Daniil Ivanovich Yuvachev stepped into the street and was instantly struck and killed by a trolleybus. He immediately regretted not looking to his left before crossing the street. Fortunately for Daniil Ivanovich, the trolleybus hit him so hard it actually knocked him back in time fifteen seconds. His foresight thus enhanced by time-displaced hindsight, Daniil Ivanovich looked left before stepping back into the street, saw the oncoming trolleybus and waited for it to pass before crossing. Unfortunately for Daniil, he neglected to look to the right and was promptly struck by a swiftly moving cube van before reaching the safety of the far curb. It can only be described as remarkable that the cube van hit him hard enough to send him back in time twenty seconds. Armed with the knowledge that he ought to look both left *and* right before crossing the street, Daniil Ivanovich managed to reach the far side of Nevsky Prospekt with his life intact. He is, however, a man both blessed and cursed with good and bad luck in equal measure, for as he stood on the sidewalk feeling quite pleased with himself, a piano fell from above and struck him on the head. Needless to say, he died almost instantly. To his continued surprise, the piano hit him so hard it knocked him back in time almost thirty seconds. Daniil Ivanovich found himself back on the sidewalk waiting to cross the street. Given everything he knew could (and still might) happen, he decided not to cross the street at all. Unfortunately, hesitation cost him dearly, for while he stood there trying to decide what to do, a PM anvil fell from above and crushed him. It was a small mercy that he died so quickly. It was, perhaps, a smaller mercy that the anvil struck him so hard it knocked him back in time forty seconds. Daniil Ivanovich was prepared this time. He turned and fled without waiting for trolleybuses or cube vans, pianos or anvils to claim his life. Life, he realized, was simply far too short to stand around. It was just rotten luck that Daniil failed to notice the open manhole. Fifty seconds later, however, he knew enough to avoid it. Unfortunately, while dodging the open manhole he ran directly into the path of a speeding bullet. The bullet pierced his heart and, quite naturally, killed him. It also struck him hard enough to knock him back in time a full sixty seconds. Daniil immediately stepped backwards. He avoided the trolleybus, the cube van, the piano, and the anvil, and because he hadn't run, he never fell through the open manhole or stepped in front of the speeding bullet. All of these things existed without his interference, and when the world seemed to settle down, he exhaled deeply and stepped around the fallen anvil only to die when an asteroid struck him. The large, extrasolar rock had been hurtling through space with such speed that when it hit Daniil Ivanovich it knocked him back in time a full sixty minutes. He found himself in bed. It was quiet and peaceful and such a blissful relief that he savoured each second of it intensely – too intensely, as it turns out. Daniil Ivanovich was so focused on the sweet silence that when his alarm clock announced the start of the day, it stopped his now fragile heart.

Those who mourned him found solace in the erroneous assumption that he died peacefully in his sleep.

Invisible Influence

de·pres·sion
/dəˈpreSH(ə)n/

noun

1. Feelings of severe despondency and dejection.
   "Self-doubt creeps in and that swiftly turns to depression"
   synonyms: melancholy, misery, sadness, unhappiness, sorrow, woe, gloom, gloominess, dejection, downheartedness, despondency, dispiritedness, low spirits, heavy-heartedness, moroseness, discouragement, despair…

Depression is much more than a simple dictionary definition. Clinical depression is a complex mood incited by everything from brain chemistry and predisposition to personality and stress. What it isn't is something that people can simply "get over". Mine is a persistent depressive disorder, something the experts call dysthymia – a chronically low mood with moderate symptoms of depression. At its worst, however, it includes a small touch of psychosis – paranoia based on beliefs that have no basis in reality. I know what you're thinking. You're expecting a story about my lifelong struggle with self-doubt. You're preparing for a melancholy tale about depression and anxiety, about how they've conspired to convince me that I'm not good enough to write. You've already predicted an ending in which I (a) recognize my self-doubt as a product of unfounded paranoia stemming from the mild psychosis of un-medicated clinical depression, and in accepting this find the emotional strength and courage to write this book, or (b) give in to the despair and gloomily vow never to write creatively again. Well slow down, sailor! Before you walk too far down that plank, let me assure you that you're wrong. True, this story does delve into self-doubt's long and often invisible influence on my life, and while depression and anxiety are featured heavily, they aren't conspiring to convince me that I'm not good enough to write. That's just ridiculous. This is a melancholy tale about depression and anxiety, about how they've conspired to convince me that I'm absolutely good enough to write. If you think about it, it just makes sense. Depression and anxiety feed on self-doubt, which in turn is nourished by despair. My writerly despair is nurtured by a baseless belief (stemming, as previously mentioned, from the mild psychosis of un-medicated clinical depression) that I can be a good writer.

I feel as though I've provided far too much in the way of introduction. On with the story!

…

…

I have to be honest with you, the whole idea that depression and anxiety have conspired against me is a little unsettling. I know, and you're right. Maybe I'm just being paranoid, but still. It's really left me feeling down. Whenever I'm feeling this downhearted, I just can't bring myself to write anything at all – even things that require little to no creative thought, like stories about fashion icon Karl Lagerfeld. I don't want to drag you down with me – you've been such great readers (pluralized because while I'm depressed I'm not without a touch of optimism) – so I think I'll just stop writing

Burma, 1942

It happened like this. The jungles to the south of us were overflowing with Japanese soldiers and I really didn't want to be captured, so I picked up my pack and said, "We should keep moving."

We'd lost Kweilin in the early morning mist and, low on fuel, had been forced to land in a narrow valley whose ownership the war had made ambiguous. Uncertain which side of that war we had landed on, Pappy and I gathered the few supplies we had and then set fire to our planes. I'd reasoned that if we found the river we could follow it back to Kweilin.

We began wending our way up the steep and narrow trail toward the northernmost ridge. We had started bickering about our predicament when, without warning, we found ourselves face-to-face with a native descending the very same trail. We three stopped with a suddenness that was almost comical. The native was small and fierce, his brown skin protected by bamboo armour.

On his chest, sheathed in bamboo, was either a really short sword or a very long knife.

He gripped the hilt and his eyes narrowed with suspicion. For a moment we simply stared at one another, silent and uncertain. Then I slowly raised my right hand in what I hoped was a friendly gesture and said, "Nice day for a stroll."

At the sound of my voice, the native slowly backed away, then turned and ran screaming back up the trail.

Pappy looked at me and said, "He must know you."

Maybe it didn't happen exactly like this. Maybe it didn't happen at all. Who's to say? The past isn't exactly etched in stone, you know.

Lost Confidence

I lost my confidence. At first, I assumed I'd just left it at home, in the dish by the door that holds my watch and wallet, my keys and loose change and such. I could picture it there, sitting at the bottom of the bowl beside two dimes and a nickel. It wasn't. I checked the minute I got home from work last night. The bowl contained nothing more than the twenty-five cents I'd left there months ago. I looked through countless pockets, drawers, and boxes. I checked behind the cushions on the couch and in the lint trap on the dryer. In short, I tore the house apart, but my confidence was nowhere to be found. To be perfectly honest, I gave up the search rather quickly, lacking the requisite confidence to continue. In no time at all I became a recluse. My vasovagal switch seemed stuck on 'flight'. I tried my best to fake it, to trick the world around me into believing I still had it, but to pull that trick off I really needed confidence. Weeks went by. I stopped writing short-but-brilliant stories (case in point) and playfully picking away at my guitar. It was then that I found the note. It was tucked between the pages of my last collection, *The Many Lives and Countless Deaths of Daniil Ivanovich*, which explains why I hadn't noticed it before. Even the smallest shred of confidence couldn't induce me to read my own writing – that would just be asking for trouble! The note was from my confidence. "Dear Jason," it began. "Things just aren't working out between us. Please understand that this is not about you. It's about me. I deserve to be confident about something that deserves confidence! I can't continue to be myself when being myself is constantly compromised by your lack of talent. Don't look for me. It's better this way. I'll find someone with the talent to support me, and without me you'll stop writing and 'playing' the guitar. I think we can both agree that would be better for pretty much everybody!" I stopped reading the note after that. It just hurt too much. For the longest time I kept waiting for a happier ending – a decent review of *The Puppet-Play of Doctor Gall*, a successfully played f-chord – a spark of newfound confidence that would, if nurtured properly, grow into something akin to the unbridled egotism of my youth. Sadly, nobody has read *Doctor Gall*, and f-chords are hard to play, so now I just sit on my couch binge-watching old episodes of *X-Files* while the dust accumulates on my empty notebooks and silent guitars.

Strawberry Milk

You're probably wondering what this story is all about. Well let me tell you! The other day I was sitting on a bench in Dieppe Park, staring across the river at Detroit's brightly lit skyline when… wait, no, that's not right. It happened in the afternoon, which means Detroit's skyline would not have been brightly lit. Come to think of it, it wasn't even Dieppe Park. That was a completely different story! Remind me to tell you all about that one later. This story has absolutely nothing to do with Dieppe Park or the Motor City's brightly lit skyline. This story's about something that happened to me just yesterday while I was visiting my parents in Windsor. We were sitting on the front porch. It was dusk and the city was quiet. My dad was smoking his pipe and the sweet tobacco smell brought a torrent of memories flooding back. I could remember…no, wait. We were sitting on the back porch, not the front. Also, it happened twelve years ago, not yesterday, and I wasn't visiting my parents in Windsor at all. I was visiting my family in Missouri. Come to think of it, there wasn't actually a porch involved either! We were sitting in the kitchen. The kids were playing Monopoly, my cousin Michael was playing the guitar and I was drinking strawberry milk straight from the bottle. We were talking about a time when we were young and we'd walked along the old railroad tracks to our uncle's filling station in Knox City. When we were kids, we agreed, life was simpler, and…wow, this is embarrassing. This story doesn't have anything to do with that! Some of the things I mentioned above did happen, but not exactly the way I described them. For example, I'm pretty sure I was in Missouri twelve years ago, the kids did play Monopoly, and I definitely drank strawberry milk straight from the bottle, but I don't think Michael played his guitar and regardless, this story isn't about that. To be honest, I'm no longer sure what it's about. Having said that, I should probably just end it here.

How They Met Themselves

I'd only just sat down when she came in. There was something ghostly about her, something oddly familiar that teased the conscious corners of my mind. Her chestnut eyes met mine as she walked past before following the *maître d'hôtel* to a small booth near the window. Their depth and loneliness left me flustered. They were Amanda's eyes. I watched her settle into the booth, remove her coat and smile up at the old man who had seated her. The smile was warm but indifferent, bookended by the same dimples I'd grown to love on Amanda's sweet face. The woman looked up, and again our eyes met, albeit briefly before I turned away. I felt a forgotten warmth rise in my cheeks.

The waitress took my order – steak medium-well with garlic mashed potatoes and a vegetable mix – and promptly vanished. My eyes remained in her wake, unfocused but for a moment before they found the woman who wasn't Amanda. She couldn't be Amanda, of course, because Amanda had died two years ago. This time her eyes found mine, and I thought I detected, perhaps not interest but curiosity, before she blushed and looked away. Even her mannerisms were reminiscent of Amanda. The way she smiled when she spoke to the waitress, the subtle tilting of her head when she listened to the day's specials. She caught me staring and I looked away.

Our eyes continued their game of tag throughout dinner. As I said, she seemed more curious than interested, though not at all angry at the attention I paid her. Midway through a second cup of coffee I felt her eyes on me. When I glanced up at her I saw an expression of melancholy thoughtfulness. Had she been Amanda, I would have sworn she was sifting through her memory, struggling to attach my face to another time and place. I shook my head, chasing the idea from my thoughts. I assured myself I was being ridiculous, that my mind was being irrationally influenced by her uncanny resemblance to my dead girlfriend. I tried ignoring her.

We finished our respective dinners at roughly the same time, which meant that we reached the door and stepped outside together. People passing us on the sidewalk could very easily have assumed we were a couple. I thought she might head for the parking lot, but instead she started walking downtown, toward the derelict shopping mall and the mundane shops and restaurants that lined the narrow-yet-busy street. I followed, not because I was pursuing her but because my house was in that same direction. When she glanced over her shoulder I saw neither fear nor anticipation in their rich brownness. I saw the same curiosity, the same sad contemplation I'd seen at the restaurant.

She stopped in front of the Capitol Theatre and I, almost subconsciously, slowed my pace. I thought about the countless times I'd taken Amanda there. The silent classics and exotic foreign features screened there were as much a part of our past as the dinners and the countless conversations we'd shared. The woman was looking at an old movie poster, or rather a new one meant to resemble its aged doppelgänger. It was a brightly coloured, highly stylized image of Buster Keaton clinging desperately to the closed tripod of an old movie camera. The thick-font words read "Buster Keaton in *The Cameraman*". Amanda loved Keaton. We both did. Aside from MGM and the Talmadge family, who didn't?

I went inside and approached the box office, acutely aware that she had followed me. The theatre itself was surprisingly, perhaps disappointingly bright. I'd hoped for the shadowed anonymity of a darkened theatre. The art deco detailing and the gilded décor, the opera boxes and the ornate ceiling only added to the room's brightness. It was a small theatre, made larger by the lack of an audience. Aside from a smattering of Damfinos and silent film aficionados, it was empty. Those who were there were sitting at orchestra level, close to the stage and eager for the film to begin. I made my way up to the deserted balcony, found a seat, not in the front row but two rows back from the railing, and sat down. She sat down beside me.

I was grateful when they dimmed the house lights and the theatre darkened. I could feel her closeness, the warmth of her body. I felt like a schoolboy on his first date, desperate for any form of physical contact yet scared shitless by the very idea of it. Neither one of us spoke. While Keaton made us both laugh, it seemed as though we were the silent film stars in our own short story – not unwilling but unable to give voice to our thoughts. We needed title cards, I thought, smiling as I did so. There was a brief intermission after which they were screening the documentary *A Hard Act to Follow*. I stood, intent on visiting the wine bar during the intermission. My throat felt dry and anxiety had fuelled my need for the calming influence of alcohol.

"Are you going to the wine bar?" Her voice sounded exactly right – that is to say exactly the way I expected it would – soft and slightly nervous. She smiled and held up a ten-dollar bill. Her hand was long and slender, pale and absolutely perfect. I wanted nothing more than to take it in mine, but instead I smiled and shook my head.

"I am, as a matter of fact. But it's my treat. What can I get you? Wait! You prefer white to red, but you're not completely sold on white wine. You want an oaked Chardonnay."

The woman laughed. "Red. Shiraz."

I blushed. I'd so irrationally convinced myself that this woman was a manifestation of Amanda that I'd made an embarrassing presumption about her taste in wine. The first words I'd given her were resounding proof of my idiocy. "I…"

She smiled and said, "Don't worry, I'm fickle and I change my mind frequently. By the time you get back here, I might actually prefer white to red and send you back to the bar for an oaked Chardonnay."

After the documentary ended we left the theatre together. We'd decided to stop at a small bar near the theatre for a nightcap, but were disappointed to find it closed. When she shrugged her slender shoulders and sighed I was afraid our evening had come to an abrupt end.

I was pleasantly surprised when she said, "I live just down the street. It's a bit of a walk, but if you want…"

"At the very least I'll walk you home," I replied. Our hands finally met and we made our way west down King Street, leaving the empty downtown lights for the quiet, tree-lined darkness of the city's old neighbourhood. It occurred to me that we hadn't exchanged names. Here we were, strolling home hand-in-hand having shared dinner and a movie and yet we knew nothing about one another. I had no desire to speak, but I wanted desperately to hear her voice, to have her tell me everything there was to know about her. The first words she spoke, ten minutes into our walk, were, "Here we are." She took a set of keys from her purse and led me up the front step to her door. Once inside, she took her shoes and coat off and went directly into the kitchen.

"Drink?" she called out.

"Scotch, please," I said. "The Aberlour." I cringed when I spoke. Again I'd made the assumption that she was Amanda's doppelgänger. "If you have it," I added somewhat weakly. I was surprised when she brought me a glass, more surprised to discover that the living room we entered was mine, lined with her artwork and my books and filled with the comforting warmth of familiarity. We sank down into the couch together and it felt so perfectly natural that I almost cried. The touch of her hip against mine, the sunflower smell of her hair, the simple sounds of the house settling and the occasional passing car left me feeling light-headed. I needed air, but at the same time I needed this. I was afraid that if I stepped outside it would disappear, and so I remained on the couch sipping my Scotch and saying nothing that would disturb the world.

The Man Nobody Knew

A man retired after forty years with the company. While my friends and I attended his retirement party we found it strange that none of us knew him. Ours was a small office and we'd all been working there for roughly twenty years each, yet not one of us recognized him. Stranger still, the man not only worked in the same office with us, he worked on the same floor and in the very same room. His desk was beside mine, and had been for at least the past decade. I've been told that he'd never missed a day of work, never took vacation and he always ate his lunch at his desk. He had been an extremely dedicated employee who'd received recognition throughout his long career for high performance. Yet when he stood to deliver his retirement speech, nobody knew who he was. I could see it on the faces of those assembled to bid him farewell – he was a complete stranger to everyone! An unspoken question followed in the wake of exchanged looks; who is this man? I leaned toward my friend and fellow co-worker and whispered, "What's his name?"

My friend nodded and whispered back, "That's exactly right."

After the retirement party, my friends and I returned to work. Our desks seemed no quieter given that we now, apparently, had one less body. Our workloads remained the same. We saw no decrease in productivity despite the loss of our alleged co-worker. At one point, I turned to one of my co-workers and asked what it was the new retiree had done for the company.

"Who?" my co-worker asked.

"What's-his-name."

My co-worker shrugged.

The day continued as days typically do, which is to say that nothing extraordinary happened. At five o'clock we left for the day. The next day began the way the previous had ended. The most extraordinary thing that happened was that my morning coffee was exceptionally good. I sat down at my desk, glanced at the empty one beside me and tried remembering the last time anyone had sat there. I couldn't. I tossed my laptop bag and coat on the vacant desk and docked my laptop on my own. Although we were required to change our passwords once every three months, I'd used the same basic format for the past six years, only changing the last digit when required. When the login screen informed me that my password was incorrect, I assumed I'd mistyped it. My second attempt failed as well, so I immediately tried the last number I remember using. My account was promptly locked. I turned to my fellow co-workers and said, "Strange, but I've managed to lock myself out."

They turned to look at me and it was as though they were seeing me for the first time. Both women stood up and introduced themselves. Women I'd worked with for at least ten years began asking me questions they should have known the answers to – about my background in marketing, my work experience and where I'd lived before moving to Chatham. It was like they didn't know me at all.

The Isle of Demons

The Isle of Demons first appeared on the 1508 map of Johannes Ruysch, a sixteenth-century explorer, cartographer, astronomer, manuscript illustrator and painter known most famously for having produced the second-oldest known printed representation of the New World. While scholars and skeptics think Ruysch merely moved the older, equally legendary island, *Satanazes* from the middle of the Atlantic to a more appropriate location, the fact of the matter is that the Isle of Demons (actually two islands separated by a narrow channel) can be found near the centre of the Ginnungagap passage between Labrador and Greenland to this day – exactly where Ruysch said it was. I know this, dear reader, because my parents used to take me and my sisters there every other summer to visit our great grandmother.

I know what you're thinking, and you're absolutely right. The island isn't on any contemporary maps, nor has it been since the mid-seventeenth century. That doesn't mean the island isn't there, it just means that the map-making heirs of Mercator, Ruysch and Ortelius simply forgot the accounts of Sebastian Cabot, Jean-Francois de la Roque de Roberval and sixteenth-century French geographer Andre Thevet. Memories are fickle. If not fed constantly, they abandon their owner to the vagaries and outright fabrications of time.

I remember my great grandmother telling us about our family's connection to the island. My sisters and I would sit on the floor at her feet while she quilted and would listen to her talk about Marguerite de la Roque's trans-Atlantic love affair with a poor sailor, and her father's rage upon discovering it. Jean-Francois was so furious, in fact, that he left Marguerite de la Roque, her lover and her servant-girl Damienne to the mercy of the beasts of our island. According to legend, Marguerite gave birth to a boy, but the child, the sailor and Damienne all died. Marguerite was eventually rescued by Basque fishermen and returned to France where she became a school teacher. Our great grandmother assured us, however, that while the sailor died, Damienne lived and raised the boy as her own. That boy married one of the island's many demons, had children of his own and so it went, so on and so forth, until my father eventually met and married my mother. When pressed for details, our great grandmother could remember little more than what she'd read in an old copy of Marguerite de Navarro's *Heptameron* and in the pages of Bellforest's *Histoires tragiques*. Our great grandmother, it turns out, was suffering from dementia and died without any memories of her own. At her funeral, I read the opening lines from George Martin's poem, *Marguerite, or The Isle of Demons*.

> You ask me, Sisters, to relate
> The story of the wanton fate
> That over sea, with dole and strife
> And love and hate enthralled my life,
> Entwined with his, whose gentle eyes,
>
> That never lost their winsome smile,
> Illumed for me those sullen skies
>
> Which canopy the haunted Isle,
> A tale so wild, I pray you think.
>
> May ill beseem and prove amiss.

When my sisters asked me what the poem meant I mentioned our summer visits to the Isle of Demons, and the stories our great grandmother used to tell us about Marguerite and Damienne.

They didn't remember any of it – not the stories, not the summer trips, not a bit of it. To this day my parents deny it. It's as if those things never happened.

Nothing Matters

I knew a man who believed in nothing. I was sceptical, of course, because I'd spent the bulk of my life believing in something. We frequently debated our philosophical differences over drinks at the local pub. He often opined that if something did, in fact, mean anything at all, it would be painfully obvious to anyone with eyes to see it and hands to touch it. On the other hand, he'd argue, nothing was all around us. Nothingness was where we came from and where we'd wind up, at which point only nothing itself mattered. Naturally I'd argue the tangible nature of the world. I would point out a chair as something, a copy of my last book as something else. "A thing isn't something simply because it exists," he'd reply. That chair isn't something. Your last book wasn't something either, it was nothing." This would invariably end our conversation. Whether we'd settled something or nothing I can't say. Stung by the idea that my last book amounted to nothing, I would make a joke about how my mother thought it was something, and then we would move on to other things. I always carry Harlequin's mask with me, and in an age of public masks and personal anonymity, I find myself less willing to remove it. I'm certain that at some point, I will simply become the person its comic visage is meant to reflect.

A Sign

People should wear signs around their neck stating their mood at any given moment in time. It could be a whiteboard so that if, while they were out and about, their mood changed they could make the necessary dry-erase adjustments. A person in a foul mood, for example, could write, "Leave me alone, I'm in a very bad mood" on their whiteboard necklace so that others would know to steer clear. Later, the fresh air having improved their frame of mind, they could change it to read, "Feeling great!" My sign would typically say, "Feeling relatively fine all things considered, although being an introvert out in public makes it difficult to remain so. In all likelihood, I'll shortly have to change this sign to better reflect the fact that my feeling fine-ish-ness is simply a façade, and a rather poor one at that. A Harlequin's mask meant to hide the ever-increasing anxiety I'm feeling in the face of (mis)perceived public scrutiny and my overwhelming fatigue at feigning smiles and polite nods in a world so caustically indifferent to itself. To be honest though, it would save time to skip any reference to social unease and go right into the depression that, when coupled with the weariness of my disquietude, manifests in a general, overriding anger that makes me completely unpleasant to be around." Or perhaps, given the limited amount of space on my whiteboard necklace I should just stay inside and sleep.

Nothing and Beingness

The very day I moved to Juan de Lisboa I ceased to exist. Of course, I didn't notice my non-existence right away. It took a few weeks to settle into my new home, to begin familiarizing myself with the culture and the customs that made island living so exotically appealing to me. I had visited islands before, but they were Caribbean islands far closer to my old Canadian home than the southern Indian Ocean.

You're probably wondering why I chose such a remote and relatively unknown island. Personally, I think the question answers itself. It's remote and relatively unknown, which means escaping the humdrum mundanity of working life has been so much easier (although I fully admit that the whole non-existence thing was both unplanned and completely unexpected). On the far side of the world, I wouldn't be tempted to visit old co-workers, have lunch with former business associates, or accidentally tread the same steps I took to and from work every business day for well over thirty years. Everything about my past life would be washed away by the endlessly rolling waves of this beautifully distant ocean. To truly appreciate my retirement decision, you need to understand that I had spent my entire life so immersed in my job that I began to consider myself a clerk first as opposed to a free human being. I lived life so utterly convinced that my job, my career, was all that I could do, all I was ever meant to do, that I never even considered doing something – anything – else. Sartre called it living in bad faith; I call it living in shackles, and while I lacked the courage to break those shackles during my working lifetime, the moment my retirement arrived, I made this leap of *good* faith.

My house was a simple beach chalet situated on Juan de Lisboa's westernmost coast – a seemingly endless stretch of white sand serenity that put every other beach I'd seen to shame. While it came furnished, I felt that perhaps the term 'furnished' lost something in translation. The small, single room contained a twin bed, a chest of drawers and what some might refer to as a kitchenette (if they were deliberately trying to mislead you). It had a roof, three walls and a wonderfully windowed façade that faced the warm, sun-kissed sea. I sat at the foot of the bed and watched that gorgeous ball of fire slip slowly beneath the soothing waves, pleasantly aware that beyond that distant horizon Madagascar, the African continent and an entirely different ocean lay between the present and the past, between personal freedom and the bad faith with which I'd lived my life, between the being and nothingness of my existence.

Juan de Lisboa was situated a few hundred miles or so from the eastern Madagascan coast – or rather it wasn't. I know that sounds confusing but if you compared Pieter Goos' seventeenth-century map of the sister islands Juan de Lisboa and Dos Romeiros with a thoroughly modern map of the southern Indian Ocean you would understand completely. I know what you're thinking. You're thinking, "Well of course I'd understand it completely because I'm a visual learner." Trust me, dear reader, it has nothing to do with your preferred learning style. It has everything to do with cartography and the observer effect. You see, Pieter Goos placed Juan de Lisboa and Dos Romeiros several hundred miles apart, and while time and various cartographers repositioned and even merged the two islands, it was Goos' map I'd referred to while planning my retirement. If I'd referenced a modern map, I would have realized that neither island actually existed – I'd have known that they only appeared on maps until the late seventeen-seventies after which they had been, as Conrad Malte-Brun's *Universal Geography* so clearly stated, declared imaginary.

The observer effect suggests that the mere observation of a phenomenon, such as a quantum state or a small island several hundred miles off the eastern coast of Madagascar, can change that phenomenon – the quantum wave function won't collapse, and the island will exist so long as they're observed. In other words, if I'd referred to Malte-Brun, a map more recently drawn than sixteen-eighty, or even a semi-reputable travel agent, maybe I'd have realized sooner that Juan de Lisboa didn't actually exist, and I never would have built my retirement plans around it. Maybe I'd have chosen someplace more realistic, like De Gama's Land or Java la Grande. The irony, of course, is that I was inspired to make this move by Sartre's *Being and Nothingness.* My pre-retirement life had been an overabundance of nothingness. By moving to Juan de Lisboa, I'd hoped for a little less 'nothing' and a little more 'being', but rather than existing as I should have all along, I stopped existing altogether.

That, as they say, is that.

Why You Should Stop Reading this Story (and Read Something by Justin Isis Instead)

This story isn't what I'd call 'good'. I wouldn't go so far as to call it terrible either, mind you. It's just that it's far too mundane to qualify as adventurous literature. I don't mean adventurous in the H. Rider Haggard sense. I mean adventurous in the refreshingly original concept sense. In short, it's all been done before. There's a protagonist. He's a struggling writer. He's down on his luck when an exotic woman enters his life. Of course she's way out of his league, but he's the protagonist so she's interested in him. The problem is, she comes with baggage – heavy baggage. She comes with ex-mobster boyfriend baggage. He gets involved because he thinks he can save her from herself. The truth is, she doesn't need saving. She's just the bait, and once he's ensnared, he's forced to ghostwrite an autobiography for the mobster, one that satisfies his all-consuming vanity. The mobster's the antagonist. He looks exactly like Al Pacino in Scarface. The woman could easily be called 'smouldering' because, of course, she is. She looks like every dangerous on-screen dame you've ever seen…with a touch of Lauren Bacall because it's my story and I've had a crush on Bacall ever since Key Largo. That doesn't make the story interesting though. That just makes it look good. The truth is, there isn't anything about this story that makes it stand out from any other unremarkable story you've ever read. Will it sell? Why not? It's got everything it needs. It's got a catchy beginning, a character-building middle and a climactic ending. It's even got a car chase! How cool is that? It has love and betrayal, steamy sex and a fist-fight with a mobster atop that pyramid hotel in Vegas. The characters can easily be compared to characters the audience has already met countless times over, and the story contains zero surprises. I mean none. There is nothing there to upset contemporary sensibilities. If you're looking for something original, something you've never read before, you should probably stop reading this story and go read something by Justin Isis. He's the real deal. If, however, you want to read about a down-on-his-luck writer who falls in love with the wrong woman and gets caught up in typical mob activity like money laundering and drug smuggling, this is definitely the place. The protagonist (his name is probably John, or Steve, or maybe Joe) even has a cute (but far from sultry) beta reader who thinks she's the next Lydia Davis (she's not, there isn't a next Lydia Davis, so get that thought right out of your head) and a gruff, hard-nosed agent who acts like he hates him but secretly loves him like a son and thinks he should write Scandinavian crime fiction despite the fact that he's not Scandinavian.

Seriously, go read Justin Isis. You've read this story a million times already.

Dead Writers

I ran into Karl Lagerfeld yesterday. I must admit I was a bit surprised given the fact that he'd died. Death aside, he looked as impeccable as ever. The funny thing about Karl was that he always wore the same thing – metallic gloves, thick tie, high-collared shirt, sunglasses and blingy accessories – yet never seemed out of style. It was a look only Lagerfeld could pull off. Trust me, I know because I've tried (more times than I can count) to wear that wonderful tie only to be mercilessly ridiculed by my co-workers. At any rate, it should come as no surprise to you that Karl and I were good friends before his unfortunate demise. As we hadn't seen one another since his funeral, we spent a few minutes catching up. We discussed everything from Italy's current fashion trends to the critical acclaim of my previous short story collection (The Many Lives and Countless Deaths of Daniil Ivanovich, Black Scat Books, 2021). Our conversations always drifted toward the written word. Both Lagerfeld and I were avid bibliophiles with ridiculously large libraries. Since the mid-eighties, we'd engaged in a bit of friendly competition over the size of our collections. During the late naughts, for a brief and glorious moment I surpassed him (fuelled by the published works of Welshman Rhys Hughes), but by 2016, Lagerfeld had reached the three hundred thousand mark, leaving me in his highly fashionable dust.

It should come as no surprise that Karl Lagerfeld and I have been good friends since the eighties. After all, we have so many things in common. We shared a passion for books, we were both undeniable fashion icons, and we were both fixtures in the world's art hubs. Donatella Versace once joked that the only way she could tell us apart is that while his work for Fendi was formal, mine was strictly pro bono consultation.

At any rate, I was surprised to see him yesterday. The most surprising thing about it wasn't that he was dead because, as I said, he looked great. No, the most surprising thing about it was that I ran into him on my way to work in Chatham-Kent, Ontario. To my knowledge, the closest Lagerfeld had ever come to Southwestern Ontario before was the bottle of Lagerfeld Cologne my dad got for Father's day back in 1979. Obviously I asked him what he was doing here. "My library," he told me, "has become a sort of gathering place for the dead writers I most admire." He went on to explain that after he'd died, he'd been given the choice between going into the light and going into his three hundred thousand volume personal library. He made the obvious choice, only to discover that his library had become overcrowded by the likes of Mallarmé, Else Lasker-Schüler and Roberto Juarroz.

"Only for the writers you admire?" I asked.

Fashion icon Karl Lagerfeld nodded. "Just yesterday I was re-reading *A Sense of Beauty* when George Santayana appeared, not out of nowhere but rather as though he'd been there the whole time. He seemed dismayed when he saw what I was reading. This – I held up the 1896 edition of his first book – is my philosophical bible. This particular edition was very hard to find. I told Santayana that it was a shame the book had never been translated into French and do you know what he said?"

It was a rhetorical question but I answered with a shake of my head nonetheless.

"He called the lack of a French translation one of life's small mercies. When I mentioned his argument that beauty is a human experience based on the senses, he shushed me. He placed a finger on my lips and actually shushed me. 'I was skirting psychologism, Herr Lagerfeld,' he said. He called the book a wretched little potboiler he'd based on a few of his old Harvard lectures, adding that he'd only written it to impress the ladies. Can you imagine? Never meet your heroes, Jason. Present company excluded, of course.

At first I wasn't sure what he meant by that, but then I noticed his footwear. He was wearing flip flops over grey wool work socks – my trademark style! He'd once confessed his hatred of sloppy footwear to me over lunch at Senequier in Saint Tropez. What he hated most, he'd said, were flip flops. He'd claimed he was physically allergic to them.

"Do the wool socks keep the allergy at bay?" I asked.

Lagerfeld laughed. "It wasn't the last time your sense of style influenced my wardrobe. I once wore camouflaged shorts to Club 55 in Ramatuelle. At any rate, my debate with Santayana did not go well. He disagreed with himself so vehemently that I simply stopped defending him. To be honest, he's all but ruined *A Sense of Beauty* for me."

"Nonsense," I said. "What does George Santayana know about *A Sense of Beauty* anyway."

"It's his book," Lagerfeld pointed out. "He wrote it."

I waved my hand dismissively. "Exactly my point, Karl. The fact that he wrote it makes him the least qualified person to explain it."

Santayana, Lagerfeld assured me, had a theory regarding the dead writers haunting the fashion icon's three hundred thousand volume home library. "When writers write – whenever artists create something from within themselves – they leave a piece of themselves behind. They impregnate their creation with the very essence of their soul."

I shrugged. Lagerfeld's revelation wasn't exactly new. "Of course," I replied. "Writers can't help but reveal themselves in their work. Whether intentional or not, their work is alive with their thoughts and opinions, their outlook on life and the world in which they wrote. Critics have known this for years! It's impossible to separate an artist from his or her work. The author can be ignored, of course. The critic can focus on the art as opposed to the artist, but it doesn't mean the artist isn't there."

Lagerfeld shook his head. "We're arguing apples and oranges, Jason. I am not talking about thoughts and opinions, or biased world views; I am talking about an author's soul. A writer's soul exists within his work. When I discussed this very thing with Santayana yesterday, he theorized that a writer's soul remains bound to the books he has written so long as they are read."

The fashion icon was right. We were talking about apples and oranges. My apple involved textual interpretation while his orange involved something far more spiritual. We decided to continue our fruitful discussion over coffee, and within minutes were sitting in my library sipping a nice light filter roast Burundi. Lagerfeld smiled as he savoured his first sip. "Delicate," he said. "Excellent balance, firm body and an almost winey cranberry taste." He took a slow, second sip and his smile broadened. "Floral, isn't it. Rose hips too, with a slightly citrus after taste."

"Spot on as usual," I replied. As an aside to this story, Karl Lagerfeld drank instant coffee before he met me. We met following a Vancouver fashion shoot. We happened to be in the same (rather long and slow-moving) line at Tim Horton's. Although we rarely ventured into the same social circles, we both skirted the outer edge of one another's, and so we recognized each other almost simultaneously. I suggested we abandon Tim Horton's in favour of the much more fashionable Lucky's Donuts, assuring Karl that the coffee served at Lucky's was far superior. It was, of course. Lucky's roasted and served direct trade coffee from the best growing regions in the world. Their in-season offerings were, and are, the best one can buy in Canada. It had since become Lagerfeld's favourite and was the only coffee I brewed at home. "Red Bourbon from the Kayanza region," I added. "So tell me more about Santayana's theory."

Lagerfeld paused, took another sip of coffee, sighed and said, "What were you reading earlier today, before you ran into me?"

"The World According to Karl," I replied, and that's when it hit me. Despite having died, Fashion Icon Karl Lagerfeld was sitting across from me, in my library, surrounded by my books and sipping coffee from one of my ceramic coffee mugs while right there, on the end table beside him, was a copy of *The World According to Karl*. The revelation shook me. If he signed the book *after* his death it would be priceless.

When I suggested he do just that, however, he said I was completely missing the point. "You ran into me having just read *The World According to Karl*. I was visited by George Santayana while reading *A Sense of Beauty*. George believes that his soul persists, that in essence he lives on after death within the bounds of my library because I still read him. The simple act of reading a dead writer's written work releases that writer's soul from the confines of each carefully chosen word to the purgatory of a library, or a bookshop – wherever one reads."

"Reading is hardly a simple act," I replied. "Or rather, it can be as simple or as complex as we want it to be, but the act of reading, of divining the myriad meanings from a text, can be an extremely complicated process."

"A poor choice of words," Lagerfeld said. "If we were characters in a story, Jason, I would question the author's word choice. Consciously or subconsciously he chose the phrase 'simple act of reading' so it must mean something."

Lagerfeld was beginning to sound like my first year English professor, walking us through his analysis of Blake's *The Sick Rose.* "If Santayana is right, that would mean the dead are tethered to the living by their own soul-embossed writing. That would make your library a purgatory for dead writers."

"Not just mine, yours as well – everywhere books are read!"

I looked around the room. My humble collection included more books by the dead than by the living, and yet I'd seen no spirits. "Where are they?" I asked. "Where are the disembodied souls of Alphonse Allais and Machado de Assis? Where are Beckett and Bloy, Kafka and Kharms? If any soul were to haunt this place, surely it would be Flann O'Brien."

Lagerfeld shrugged. "Yet here I am, a dead man haunting your library mere hours after you finished reading *The World According to Karl*. It was Santayana, remember, who reached out to me, and it was I who reached out to you. Perhaps the dead must instigate; perhaps O'Brien has nothing to say."

I thought about it, and while I couldn't dispute the fact that I was having coffee with a dearly departed fashion icon whose book of witticisms I'd only just finished reading, there were so many other implausibilities at play I still found Santayana's theory difficult to swallow. "Where do you go when you aren't here?" I asked.

Lagerfeld picked up my copy of *The World According to Karl* and said, "This book is such a small contribution to my legacy, Jason. The ties that bind my soul to this world are more likely actual ties." He flipped his extremely wide tie in an Oliver Hardy-like manner. "I am bound more by my aesthetic than by my words, but the result is the same. Whenever someone visits my website, buys my clothes or recalls my contribution to the world of high fashion, I am pulled unwaveringly toward them."

"You have no choice?"

"No, the choice is theirs, not mine. If I ignored the great expressionist poetess Else Lasker-

Schüler's presence within her work, choosing instead to focus on the work itself, I would not see her, I could not commune with her. By ignoring the artist I would be ignoring the emotion, the true passion in the poem. It would be a dead work, limited to the mere mechanics of form. I would, in short, cut myself off from the deeper and far more beautiful aspects of the poetry – the poetess herself!"

Hemingway, whom I've spoken to often since Lagerfeld's first visit, once said, "There is nothing to writing. You just sit down at the typewriter and bleed." That is precisely what I began doing the moment Lagerfeld left that day. I bled my heart and soul into every single word I wrote. I ignored ambiguity and made sure my thoughts and feelings were evident in each and every one of my stories. Throughout my remaining years I met countless dead writers, from Allais (who didn't speak a word of English) to Zoshchenko (who didn't speak a word of English either). I once debated the term magical realism with two of its progenitors – Borges and Bombal, and learned more than I ever cared to know about Corvo's final days in Venice.

Through it all I wrote. I bled, as Hemingway said, until I knew I had nothing left to give. I bled myself dry, and on that day I died.

Before I met Karl Lagerfeld I was terrified of death, of its uncertainty. Forty years had passed since that coffee-infused conversation, and in that time I'd become almost eager for death. As a living writer, I rarely discussed my writing with anyone. I would have loved to, mind you, but nobody ever brought it up. In death I could reach out to those still-living readers to talk about the stories I'd written. I'd explain that while they appeared whimsical and frivolous they were actually driven by depression and crippling self-doubt, that I used humour to mask a sadness that at times felt overwhelming.

But now that I am dead I've come to fear it again. I've heard from no one. Nobody reads my work. Nobody remembers. The living have forgotten me entirely and so death really is...

The End.

Jason E. Rolfe is the author of three novellas, *The Puppet-Play of Doctor Gall* (Black Scat Books), *An Archive of Human Nonsense* (Snuggly Books) and *Synthetic Saints* (Vagabondage Press); as well as two short story collections for Black Scat Books, *The Many Lives and Countless Deaths of Daniil Ivanovich* and *Clocks*. His short stories have appeared in *Uncertainties V* (Swan River Press), *Ghost Trains* (Raphus Press), *Bitter Distillations* (Egaeus Press), *The Neo-Decadent Cookbook* (Eibonvale) and *Le Scat Noir Encyclopédie et Dictionnaire de la Pataphysique* (Black Scat Books). Jason lives in Southwestern Ontario, Canada.

www.ingramcontent.com/pod-product-compliance
Lightning Source LLC
Chambersburg PA
CBHW030845200726

48285CB00007B/2555